EARLY BIRD STORIES™

My Family Celebrates
KWANZAA

Lisa Bullard

Illustrated by Constanza Basaluzzo

LERNER PUBLICATIONS ◆ MINNEAPOLIS

NOTE TO EDUCATORS

Find text recall questions at the end of each chapter. Critical-thinking and text feature questions are available on page 23. These help young readers learn to think critically about the topic by using the text, text features, and illustrations.

Lerner Publications Company
A division of Lerner Publishing Group, Inc.
241 First Avenue North
Minneapolis, MN 55401 USA

For reading levels and more information, look up this title at www.lernerbooks.com.

Photos on page 22 used with permission of: Timothy R. Nichols/Shutterstock.com (candles); hlphoto/Shutterstock.com (corn); Vstock LLC/Getty Images (cup).

Main body text set in Billy Infant 22/28.
Typeface provided by SparkyType.

Library of Congress Cataloging-in-Publication Data

Names: Bullard, Lisa, author. | Basaluzzo, Constanza, illustrator.
Title: My family celebrates Kwanzaa / Lisa Bullard ; illustrated by Constanza Basaluzzo.
Description: Minneapolis : Lerner Publications, 2019. | Series: Holiday time (Early bird stories) | Includes bibliographical references and index. | Audience: Age 5-8. | Audience: K to grade 3.
Identifiers: LCCN 2017049352 (print) | LCCN 2017056392 (ebook) | ISBN 9781541525009 (eb pdf) | ISBN 9781541520110 (lb : alk. paper) | ISBN 9781541527423 (pb : alk. paper)
Subjects: LCSH: Kwanzaa—Juvenile literature. | African Americans—Social life and customs—Juvenile literature.
Classification: LCC GT4403 (ebook) | LCC GT4403 .B855 2019 (print) | DDC 394.2612—dc23

LC record available at https://lccn.loc.gov/2017049352

Manufactured in the United States of America
1-44347-34593-12/28/2017

TABLE OF CONTENTS

CHAPTER 1

READY FOR KWANZAA

Hi! I'm Kevin. We're getting ready for Kwanzaa.

That's a special holiday for my family. It celebrates our African American culture.

My mom puts a mat on a table. I add the candleholder and candles. Mom adds fruits and vegetables.

Next comes the unity cup. We put out presents too!
Now we're ready for Kwanzaa.

What holiday
is Kevin's family
getting ready for?

CHAPTER 2

LIGHTING THE CANDLES

Kwanzaa lasts for seven days. We light another candle each night.

My grandpa goes first. Tonight he lights the black candle.

Then Grandpa explains the Kwanzaa word for the first day. Every day has a special word in Swahili. That's an African language.

Nguzo Saba
The Seven Principles

Umoja = Unity

Kujichagulia = Self-Determination

Ujima = Collective Work and Responsibility

Ujamaa = Cooperative Economics

Nia = Purpose

Kuumba = Creativity

Imani = Faith

Grandpa's word means "unity." That means sticking together as a group.

Sticking together is why Kwanzaa began. A man named Dr. Maulana Karenga created Kwanzaa in 1966.

He wanted to bring African Americans together.

How many days does Kwanzaa last?

CHAPTER 3

ANOTHER WORD EACH NIGHT

Somebody new lights the candles each night. I watch closely so I'm ready for my turn.

Mom lights the candles
on the third night.

We talk about helping
one another solve
problems.

My brother lights the candles on the fifth night.
We talk about setting goals to help our community.

My goal is to be a teacher!

The sixth night of Kwanzaa is my favorite.

We go to a big party every year.

Who lights the candles on the third night?

19

CHAPTER 4

MY TURN!

It's the last day of Kwanzaa. I finally get to light the candles!

Grandpa says my special word means "faith."
He says I should believe in our people every day.
That will be like living Kwanzaa all year long!

Nguzo Saba
The Seven Principles

Umoja = Unity

Kujichagulia = Self-Determina

Ujima = Collective Work and
Responsibility

Ujamaa = Cooperative Econo

Nia = Purpose

Kuumba = Creativity

ni = Faith

What does
Kevin's special
word mean?

LEARN ABOUT HOLIDAYS

Kwanzaa lasts from December 26 to January 1. Each day stands for a different Kwanzaa word, such as "unity" or "faith."

The Kwanzaa candleholder has three red candles, three green candles, and one black candle. The candles are lit in a special order.

Families celebrate Kwanzaa in many ways. Some families drink juice from a special unity cup.

In the 1950s and 1960s, many people worked hard to make the lives of African Americans better. Dr. Maulana Karenga created Kwanzaa during this time.

Fruits and vegetables are important during Kwanzaa. They remind people of the old celebrations held in Africa when the crops were ready.

THINK ABOUT HOLIDAYS: CRITICAL-THINKING AND TEXT FEATURE QUESTIONS

Why was Kwanzaa created?

Why do you think Kwanzaa lasts for seven days?

What chapter starts on page eight?

Where is the glossary in this book?

LERNER
e
SOURCE™

Expand learning beyond the printed book. Download free, complementary educational resources for this book from our website, www.lernerresource.com.

GLOSSARY

African American: someone or something that has both an African and an American background

candleholder: something that is made to hold candles

culture: shared beliefs, language, foods, and other things that define a group of people

faith: believing in someone or something

goal: something you work to achieve

TO LEARN MORE

BOOKS
Herrington, Lisa M. *Kwanzaa.* New York: Children's Press, 2014. Learn about the history and traditions of Kwanzaa in this easy read-aloud book.

Washington, Donna L. *Li'l Rabbit's Kwanzaa.* New York: Katherine Tegen Books, 2010. Join Li'l Rabbit as he searches for a Kwanzaa gift for his grandmother.

WEBSITE
Activity Village
https://www.activityvillage.co.uk/kwanzaa
Play games, find coloring pages, and learn more about Kwanzaa on this website.

INDEX